Unicorn
Sparkle & Shine!
Coloring and Activity Book

Silver Dolphin

When unicorns wake up, they bow to the sun.

A bath in a waterfall is the perfect way to start the day.

Hey! No splashing!

Unicorns dry off with soft, warm towels.
Decorate this one with flowers.

5

It's time to braid tails and manes!

Draw lines between the matching bows.

Curls are a very cute look!

Fresh berries and rainbow ice cream sundaes are a perfect snack!

Find the two sundaes that are the same.

See page 79 for answer.

Which butterfly comes next in each row?

A   B   B   A   B   _____

A   A   B   B   A   _____

A   B   A   B   A   _____

See page 79 for answers.

Write the letters of the missing "puzzle pieces" in the squares to complete the scene.

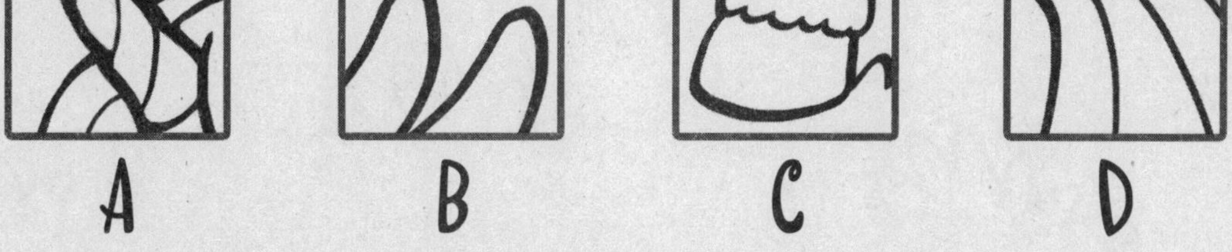

A

B

C

D

See page 79 for answers.

15

It's time to frolic with butterflies . . .

...and have a game of tag with dragonflies!

Sometimes the bumblebees whisper secrets.

See page 79 for answer.

Draw a unicorn playing with friends.

Hopscotch with bunnies is a lot of fun!

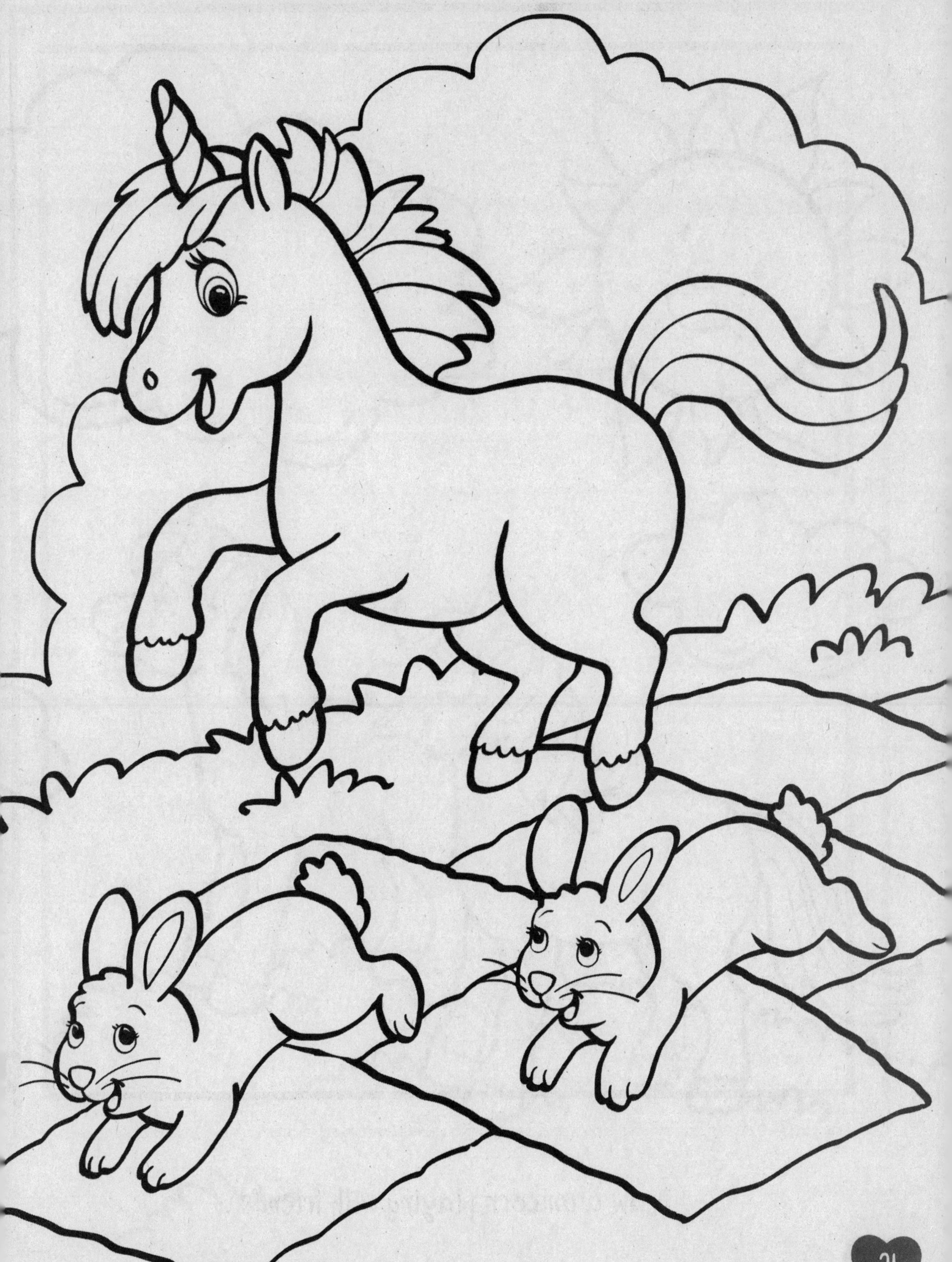

Look! The alicorns are flying in to see their unicorn cousins.

Alicorn wings are beautiful, and each pair is different.

It's time for a unicorn party—with cupcakes, of course!

Find and circle the cupcake that is different.

See page 79 for answer.

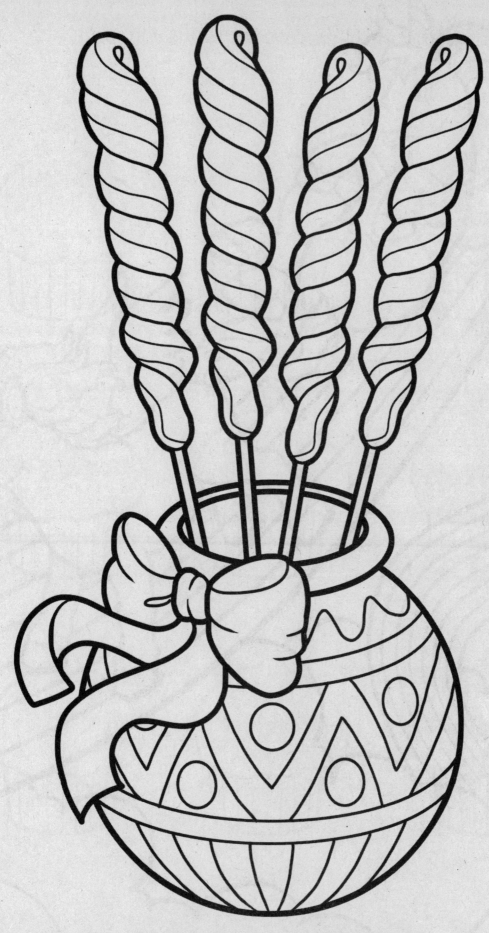

Yum! Rainbow unicorn lollipops!

The rainbow races are underway! Who will win the trophy?

Unicorns love seeing rainbows!

30

Get the unicorn to the rainbow!

Finish

Start

See page 79 for answer.

31

Draw a line to match the image of the unicorn to its shadow.

See page 79 for answers.

Friends can share ivy garlands.

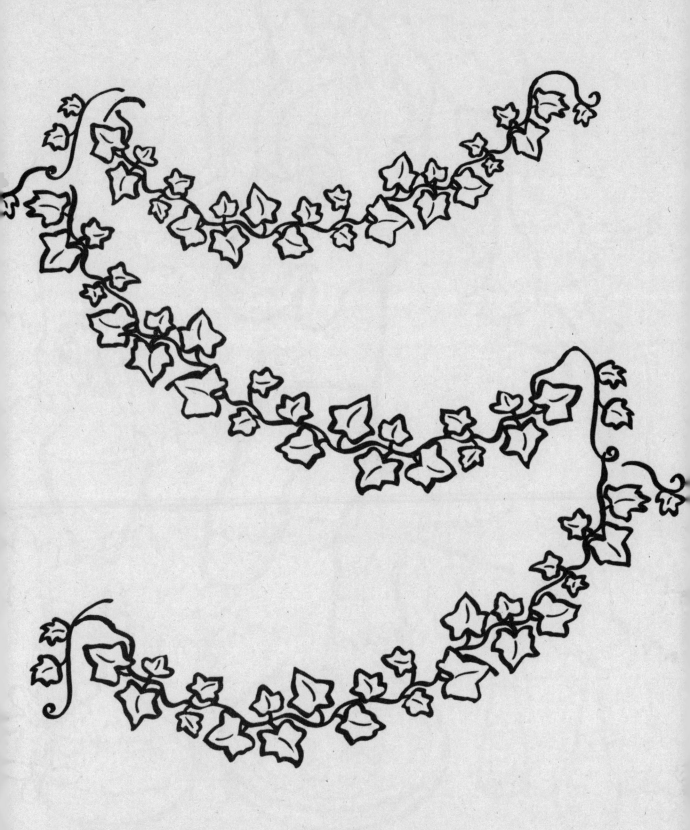

Decorate the ivy garlands with flowers or
hearts—or whatever looks pretty!

What a treat to go to the spa and get your hooves painted!

Which path should the unicorn take to get to the spa?

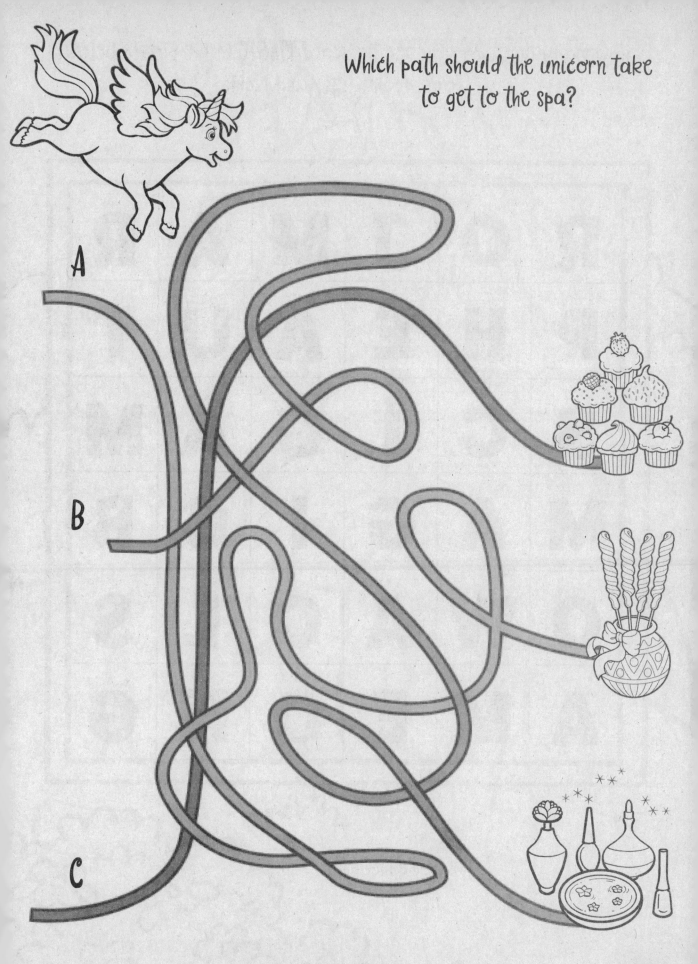

A

B

C

See page 79 for answer.

37

How many times do you see the word MAGIC in the puzzle below?
Look down, left, and right.

R	O	J	M	A	R
P	H	E	A	U	T
S	C	I	G	A	M
M	A	G	I	C	B
O	W	A	C	L	S
A	M	E	O	N	G

See page 80 for answer.

Ring toss! What a perfect use of a unicorn horn!

How's this for a
balancing trick?

40

Draw something else the unicorn can balance on her horn.

Every unicorn is special.
This one is striped!

Draw a line to match each unicorn to its twin.

See page 80 for answers.

43

Some unicorns have spots and some have hearts.

Some have stars and some have paisley markings.

Decorate this unicorn with a pretty pattern.

A unicorn's most prized feature is its beautiful horn!

Unicorns touch horns to greet each other.

How many times do you see the word **UNICORN** in the puzzle below?
Look up, down, left, right, and diagonally.

R	O	J	U	A	R	U
C	M	W	N	E	N	N
S	U	T	I	I	L	R
P	H	E	C	A	B	O
O	W	O	O	L	S	C
K	R	E	R	M	G	I
N	P	F	N	T	R	N
N	R	O	C	I	N	U

See page 80 for answer.

49

Everyone gets dressed up for the Unicorn Ball.
Just look at this tiara!

Dress your unicorn for a ball.
Use some of the items below for inspiration!

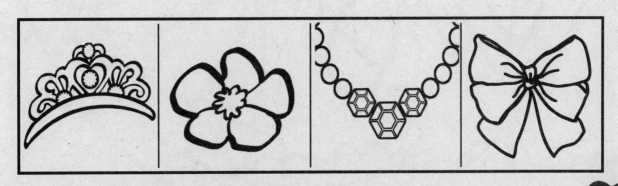

How do you like this tutu?

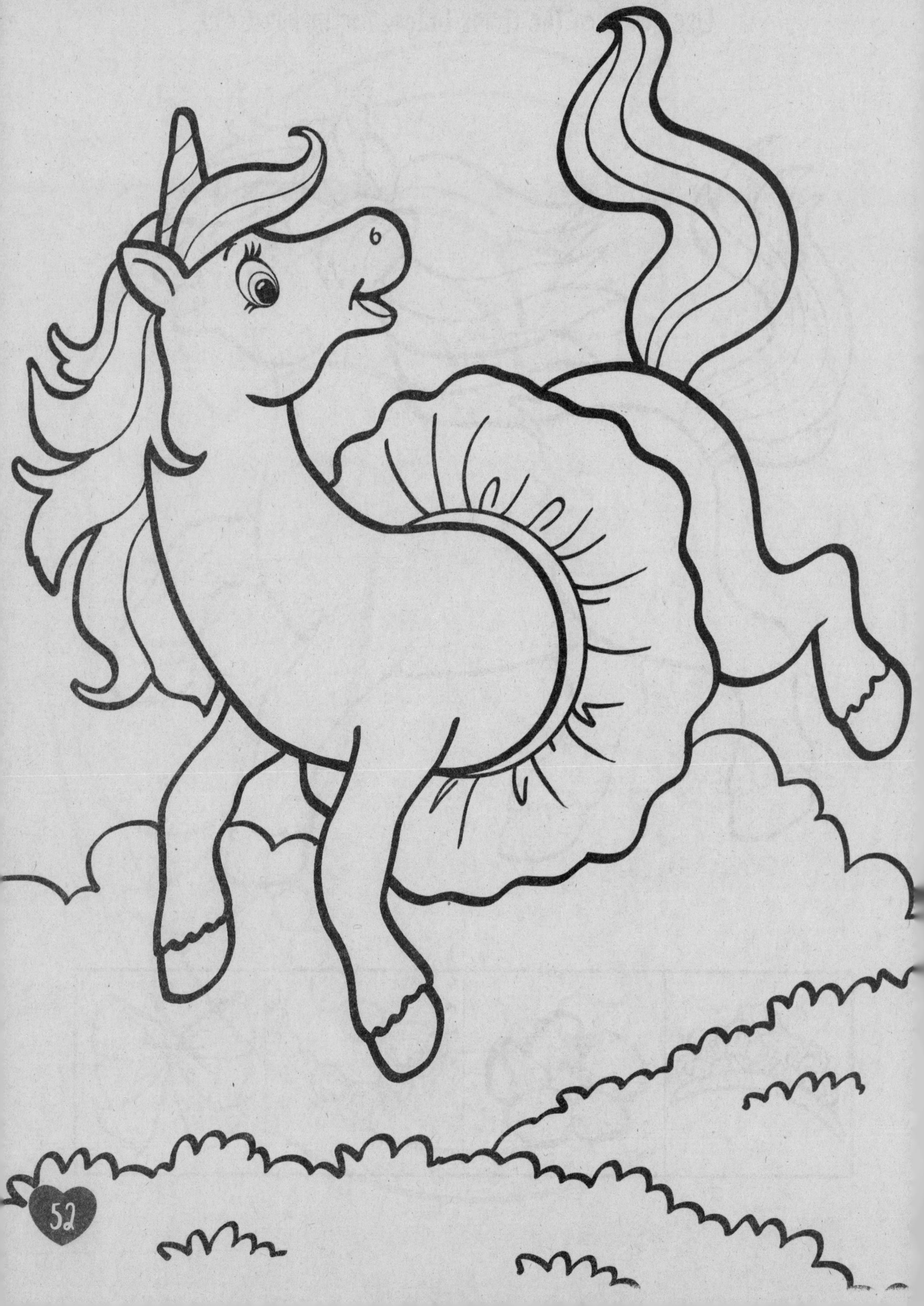

What a beautiful necklace!

Finish this necklace by adding jewels.
Use the images below for inspiration!

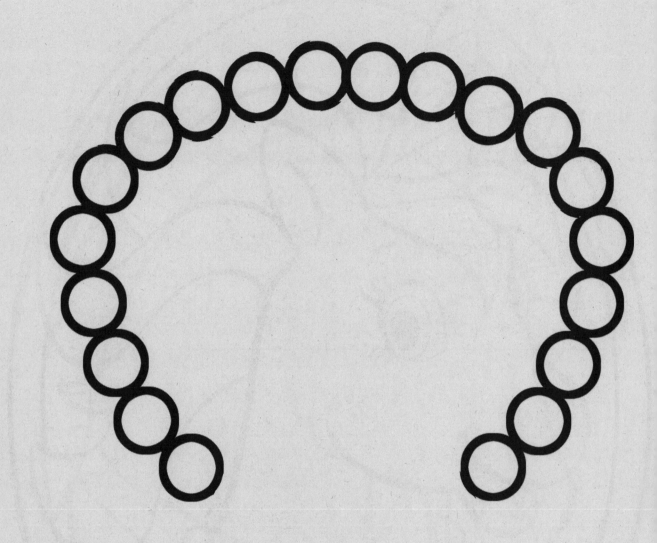

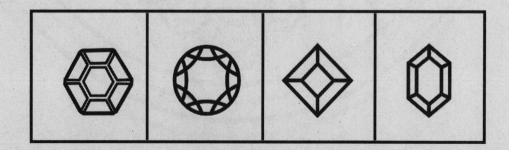

A gentleman unicorn wears his finest tux.

At the Unicorn Ball, everyone heads
straight to the dance floor!

The decorations are delightful!

57

This unicorn is performing a special ballet!

Follow the hoofprints to help the unicorn find her dance partner.

Start

Finish

See page 80 for answer.

59

The musicians play lively tunes.

The night ends with a dazzling fireworks display!

A baby unicorn is called a sparkle.

These sparkles are getting sleepy!

Sparkles sleep on rainbow beds with cloud pillows.

Follow the path between the clouds to get the sparkle to her cloud pillow.

Finish

Start

See page 80 for answer.

67

This sparkle is dreaming of a narwhal!

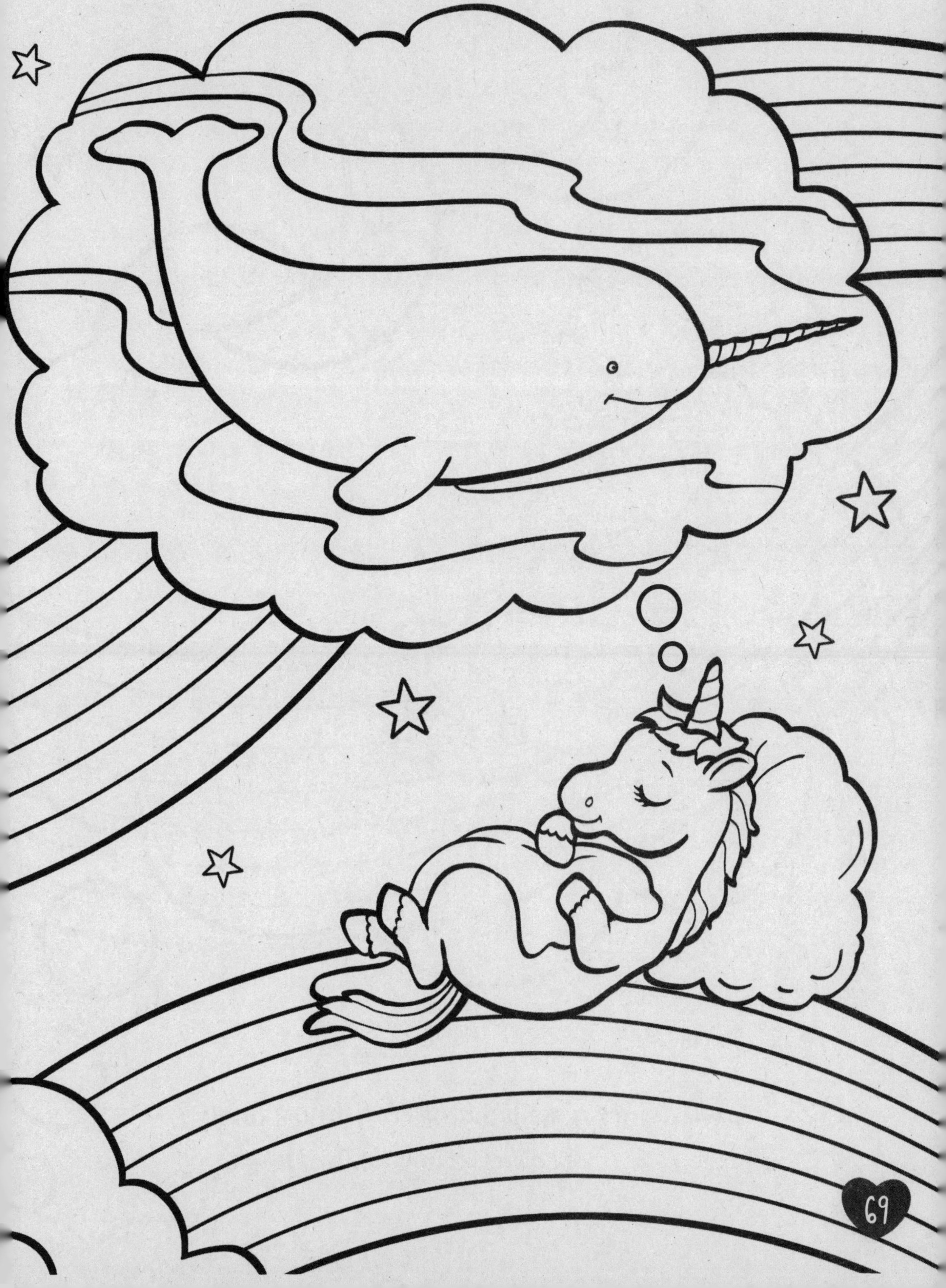

What does your baby unicorn dream about?
Draw a picture of it.

70

All too soon, it is time to say goodbye to the alicorns.

To get home, the alicorns ride on shooting stars.

Connect the dots to complete the picture.

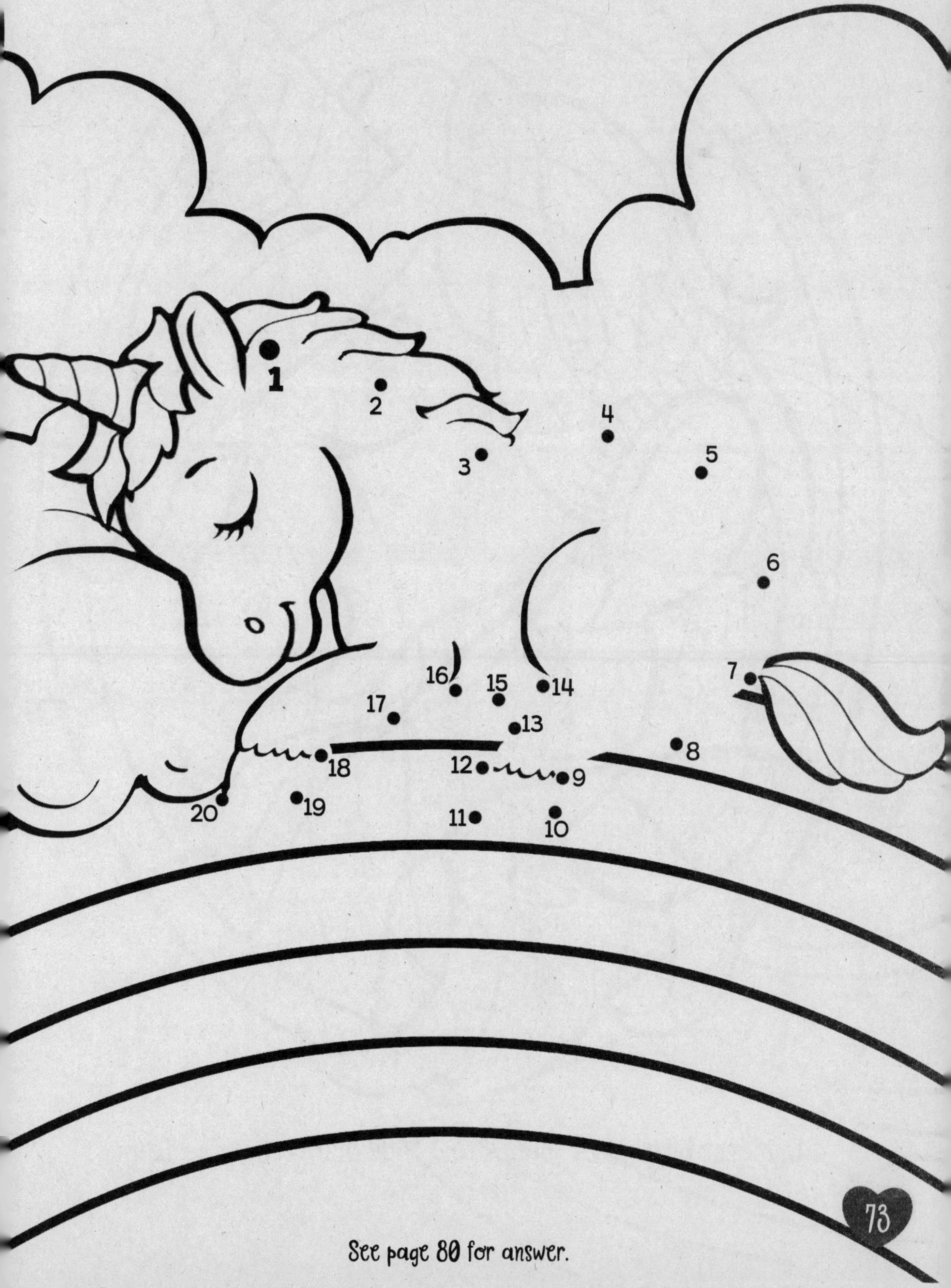

1
2
3
4
5
6
7
8
9
10
11
12
13
14
15
16
17
18
19
20

See page 80 for answer.

Unicorns brush their manes and tails before they go to bed.

... and blow kisses to the moon.

Then they go to sleep.

ANSWERS

Page 10

Page 13

Page 14

Page 15

K I N D N E S S

I S   Y O U R

M A G I C

Page 19

Page 26

Page 31

Page 32

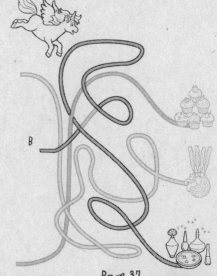

Page 37

ANSWERS

3 times

R	O	J	**M**	**A**	**R**
P	H	E	**A**	U	T
S	**C**	**I**	**G**	**A**	**M**
M	**A**	**G**	**I**	**C**	**B**
O	W	A	**C**	L	S
A	M	E	O	N	G

Page 38

Page 43

4 times

R	O	J	**U**	**A**	**R**	U
C	M	W	**N**	**E**	**N**	N
S	U	T	**I**	**I**	**L**	R
P	H	E	**C**	**A**	**B**	O
O	W	**O**	**O**	**L**	S	C
K	**R**	**E**	**R**	M	G	I
N	P	F	N	T	R	N
N	R	O	C	I	N	U

Page 49

Page 59

Page 67

Page 73